Dear Parent:
Your child's love of reading starts here!

I Can Read Books have introduced children to the joy of reading since 1957. Featuring award-winning authors and illustrators and a fabulous cast of beloved characters, I Can Read Books set the standard for beginning readers. From books your child reads with you to the first books they read alone, there are I Can Read Books for every stage of reading:

SHARED READING
Basic language, word repetition, and whimsical illustrations, ideal for sharing with your emergent reader

BEGINNING READING
Short sentences, familiar words, and simple concepts for children eager to read on their own

READING WITH HELP
Engaging stories, longer sentences, and language play for developing readers

READING ALONE
Complex plots, challenging vocabulary, and high-interest topics for the independent reader

ADVANCED READING
Short paragraphs, chapters, and exciting themes for the perfect bridge to chapter books

Every child learns in a different way and at their own speed. Some read through each level in order. Others go back and forth between levels and read favorite books again and again. You can help your young reader improve and become more confident by encouraging their own interests and abilities.

A lifetime of discovery begins with the magical words, **"I Can Read!"**

For Maddie
—L.S.

To Sosha,
who just lost another tooth
—S.W.

HarperCollins®, 🐟®, and I Can Read Book® are trademarks of HarperCollins Publishers Inc.

Library of Congress Cataloging-in-Publication Data
Schaefer, Lola M.
  Loose tooth / by Lola M. Schaefer ; pictures by Sylvie Wickstrom.—1st ed.
    p.   cm. — (My first I can read book)
  Summary: A young child experiences a loose tooth for the first time and eagerly waits for it to come out.
  ISBN 0-06-052776-5 — ISBN 0-06-052777-3 (lib. bdg.) — ISBN 0-06-052778-1 (pbk.)
  [1. Teeth—Fiction. 2. Stories in rhyme.] I. Wickstrom, Sylvie, ill. II. Title.
III. Series.
PZ8.3.S289Lo 2004
[E]—dc21
                                                                2003006322

❖

MY FIRST
I Can Read Book®

Loose Tooth

story by **Lola M. Schaefer**
pictures by **Sylvie Wickstrom**

🎞 HarperCollins*Publishers*

It's loose.

It's loose.

My tooth is loose!

I can see it.

I can feel it.

I can pull it.

I can push it.

But it won't come out!

It's loose.

It's loose.

My tooth is loose!

I wiggled it for Brother.

I wiggled it for Mom.

I wiggled it for Sister,

and my good friend Tom.

But it won't come out!

It's loose.

It's loose.

19

My tooth is loose!

I just ate an apple.

I bit a hard nut.

I chewed a long carrot.

And—guess what?

My tooth is loose,

loose,

loose.

But it won't come out!

Brother says, "Pull it!"

Sister says, "Wait."

Dad says, "Let's see."

Mom says, "Too late!"

My tooth came out

with NO help from me.

Now there's a hole
where my tooth
used to be!